In Trouble *Again*, Zelda Hammersmith?

Also by Lynn Hall

Zelda Strikes Again!
Here Comes Zelda Claus
   and Other Holiday Disasters
Flyaway
The Solitary
If Winter Comes
Mrs. Portree's Pony
The Giver
Tazo and Me

Lynn Hall

In Trouble *Again,*
Zelda Hammersmith?

Harcourt Brace Jovanovich, Publishers
San Diego   New York   London

Requests for permission to make copies of any
part of the work should be mailed to:
Permissions Department,
Harcourt Brace Jovanovich, Publishers,
Orlando, Florida 32887.

Library of Congress Cataloging-in-Publication Data
Hall, Lynn.
In trouble again, Zelda Hammersmith?
Summary: Five episodes in the zany life of fourth-
grader Zelda Hammersmith, in which she deals with a
bad report card, a boy who does not want to be her
boyfriend, the loss of her best friend, and other
tribulations.
  [1. Humorous stories] I. Title.
PZ7.H1458In 1987 [Fic]   87-8489
ISBN 0-15-238780-3

Designed by Nancy Ponichtera
Printed in the United States of America
B C D E

Contents

1. Bug On, Zelda

I've been having a little trouble lately with my love life.

It's my first love-life trouble.

Well, it's my first love life.

The trouble started the day I climbed to the top of the army tank.

I'd been wanting to climb it ever since they parked it there, in the back lot behind the National Guard Armory, next door to where I live. I live in Perfect Paradise Trailer Park, at the edge of town.

The armory has a lot of neat stuff behind it—jeeps, and a cannon, and this one huge tank parked right beside the back fence. The tank was the highest thing around, so naturally I climbed it.

Sitting on the very top, I could see across the fence and down into somebody's backyard . . . and there he was. The boy of my dreams.

He looked beautiful. He had straight black hair like a crow's tail, and deep dark dangerous eyes.

He was playing with a big dog. He'd throw a stick for it and then chase the stick himself because the dog didn't give a fat rat about chasing sticks.

I watched him for a long time. Then I went home for lunch and advice.

Mom was at work, so lunch and advice had to come from Mrs. Birdsall, who watches out for me and feeds me lunch.

Mrs. Birdsall lives in the trailer next to ours. She's the skinniest lady in the world, and she suffers from her sinus. That's her main hobby.

I sat down in her dinette booth and

ate the chicken salad that is her idea of lunch. I don't think she's ever heard of peanut butter.

She stood over me, pinching the bridge of her nose and asking me if I ever have sinus.

"I've got something worse," I told her. She looked at me like nothing could be worse than sinus.

"I'm in love," I explained.

That made her sit down, boy.

"With whom?" she said.

"I don't know his name yet." I polished off the last of the salad. "Mrs. Birdsall, am I beautiful, would you say?" I went to the mirror on the bathroom door and tried to decide.

"Little girls shouldn't ask questions like that," she said. I figured she'd come out with something like that.

I thought I was beautiful. Well, maybe pretty. Well, maybe cute. I was built like a brick. Lots of curly hair the color of cookie dough at sunset. Steely eyes and a determined chin.

Mom told me I had a determined chin. I asked her what was it determined to do—hold up my teeth? She didn't have an answer.

Poor Mom. That happens to her a lot.

I should have known better, but I asked Mrs. Birdsall for advice.

"How do I make a boy like me?" I asked her.

"To have a friend, be a friend," she said. "Honesty is the best policy," she added and finished off with "A friend in need is a friend indeed."

"A bird in the hand will peck your knuckle," I shot back, but she didn't get it.

"Where are you going, dear?" she asked as I jumped her front steps and started down the road.

"To be a friend. Indeed."

She didn't get that, either.

ↄ

I had to walk up and down his street all afternoon, but finally he came out and got on his bike and headed toward me.

Honesty is the best policy, I told myself, and leaped out in front of him.

"My name is Zelda Hammersmith," I said, "and I'm your new girlfriend."

That's when he ran his bike into a trash can and fell off at my feet.

"Who are you?" he asked, like I was something rotten in the garbage. But up close he was even more beautiful than he was from afar. Oh, those deep dark dangerous eyes!

Honesty is the best policy.

"I'm your new girlfriend," I repeated. "Zelda Hammersmith."

He picked himself up from the trash and pulled a grapefruit rind out of his spokes.

"Bug off, Zelda," he said.

He started pedaling, so I had to run along beside his bike. It's hard to pour out your love when you're puffing for breath.

"Have you already got a girlfriend?" I asked.

"No, and I haven't got an earache either. Or the flu. Or a sunburn on the top of my head, or . . ."

I got the picture.

He paused at the corner, and I had enough breath left to try another angle. "Do your parents think you're too young to have a girlfriend? This is your chance to prove they're wrong!"

I figured that would be irresistible.

He resisted.

"Bug off, Zelda," he said.

"Be the first one of your friends to go steady. Show them you're more mature than they are."

"Bug *off*, Zelda."

He started pedaling again.

"I like your dog," I yelled as a last resort when I couldn't keep up any longer.

That got him. He stopped.

"He's a purebred otter hound. Got

a pedigree as long as your arm."

I looked down at my arm. "Well, he did look like an odder hound. What's a pedigree?"

"It's his ancestors. All famous champions."

"What's his name?"

"Phil."

"Your dog's name is Phil?"

"Yeah. You want to make something out of it?"

I shook my head. "What's your name?"

"Nathanial."

Nathanial. It was a beautiful name. It went right to my heart and curled up there.

"Nathanial what?" I asked.

"Gorsuch, if you want to know."

"Of course I want to know. That's why I asked. How can I send you valentines and stuff like that if I don't know your whole name?"

He sort of groaned and pedaled off, fast.

"If you send me valentines I'll break your face," he yelled.

"But I love you," I yelled back.

His parting words came floating back from half a block away.

"Bug off, Zelda."

But Zelda Hammersmith never gives up. I was determined to bug *on*.

℮

Mom and I have been living in our trailer ever since Pop ran off to Nashville to make it big as a country western singer. That was ages ago, so I don't remember him. Mom says sometimes it takes years—or forever—to make it big in Nashville.

Mom is a good old mom. She has my same build only more so, and great big muscles, especially around her stomach. She works as a sausage stuffer in a meat-packing plant.

That night when she asked me what I did all day, I told her.

"Cleaned my room, climbed the tank, fell in love. . . ."

Naturally she wanted to know all about Nathanial. "How old is he?" That was her first question.

"Older than me. He's probably got a double-digit age on him," I said.

She nodded and looked interested even though she was cooking supper. That's how you can tell a good mom.

While I set the table, I told her everything I knew about Nathanial. It didn't take long.

"So how should I make him love me?" I asked at the end of my story.

"Tear up the lettuce for salad."

"That will make Nathanial love me?"

"No, but it will give us some salad with our supper."

"I had salad for lunch," I said.

"A little health never hurt anyone."

I made the salad.

When we were finally sitting and eating, Mom put on her wise look and said, "Offhand I think your big mistake with Nathanial is that you're chasing him."

"How else am I going to catch him?"

"No, no, dumpling, you don't understand how it works."

I hate it when she calls me dumpling. As soon as I hear that word I start feeling fat. And like I said before, I'm not fat. I'm just . . . sturdy. Except when Mom calls me dumpling; then I blow up like biscuits in a hot oven.

"This is how it works," she explained. "You have to let him chase you. See, men are hunters by nature. They like capturing the prize. They don't like *being* the prize."

"That's easy to say, but how do I get him to chase me?"

"Well," she said, "that's the tricky part."

"I know," I yelled.

"Simmer down, Zelda." That was her warning voice, so I simmered down.

"You get him to chase you," she said

more pleasantly, "by playing hard to get. Make him think you're not all that interested in him because you have so many other boys on the string."

"What other boys?" I asked darkly.

Mom just shrugged. "That's your problem."

"Aren't you going to help me?"

"Meeting challenges will be a growth experience for you."

I hate it when she says things like that—like "Look it up; you'll remember it longer."

But this time I decided there was some wisdom in Mom's advice. One way or another, I was going to have to get Nathanial to chase me.

It wasn't going to be easy.

℮

First I tried staying away from Nathanial. I stayed away all morning. The trouble was, he didn't *know* I was staying away because I was busy with so many other boyfriends.

So I tried walking past his house, but on the other side of the street. I thought that might get the message to him. He wasn't anywhere in sight.

At about three o'clock, he finally came out and headed toward me, walking Phil on a leash. I got all excited, thinking it was starting to work, and he was coming after me.

I took Mom's advice about letting him chase me. I turned around and started in the other direction, walking slowly so he could catch up with me.

Finally, when I couldn't stand it any longer, I peeked to see if he was getting close.

He wasn't anywhere in sight.

"Come on, Nathanial," I yelled, "you're not playing this right."

I backtracked, but I never did find him.

Okay, I said to myself, *this calls for desperate measures.*

I went back to Perfect Paradise and got Derek. He lives in the second trailer on the right. He's younger than me, but at least I knew he'd do whatever I told him.

"You're going to pretend to be my boyfriend," I said to him.

"Oh, no, I'm not."

"Come on, Derek. You have to."

"No, I don't."

What a time for him to start getting tough. He'd never stood up to me before.

"Okay then, will you *please* help me?"

He thought about it. "What do I have to do, and what will you pay me?"

"What happened to friendship, Derek?" I was hurt.

"Money's better," he said.

I tried to appeal to his heart, but after a while I decided he didn't have one. So I offered him the eight dollars I was saving from my birthday money.

"What do I have to do?" he grumbled.

"Just act out a part, like you would

in a play. I'll tell you your lines, and you say them. But you have to be really good at it, like a real actor. You have to sound like you mean it. Do you think you can do that?"

"For eight dollars I can."

We went down to the end of the trailer park, where there were trees and a picnic table. We had the place to ourselves, since grown-ups always think it's too hot to be outside on summer afternoons. That was fine with me. They got to use the world most of the time.

We sat on top of the picnic table, and I gave Derek his lines.

"I'll say, 'Bug off, Derek, I'm not interested in you. You're too young and boring.' And then you say, 'Zelda, I love you, I love you! You're so wonderful and beautiful.' Or something like that."

Derek looked like he was about to throw up. "I have to say that? Out loud? Where somebody might hear me?"

"Somebody is supposed to hear you, stupid. That's the whole point of this.

How can I make him jealous if he doesn't hear you? Come on, now. I'll say my line, and you say yours. Bug off, Derek, I'm not interested in you. You're too young and boring."

He waited an awfully long time, but finally he said in his lowest voice, "Zelda, I love you, I love you. You're beautiful and wonderful. When do I get my eight dollars?"

"After the performance. That was just the rehearsal. And you're going to have to be a lot more convincing than that. And a lot louder."

ℰ

Nathanial didn't come into his backyard any more that afternoon. I watched from the top of the tank till suppertime. Meanwhile, Derek sat halfway down the tank, on top of the treads, complaining.

First he said he couldn't climb to the top with me because when his great-grandma was dying, he'd promised her he'd never climb anything higher than his head.

Derek lies a lot.

Then he told me I'd get arrested for climbing the tank because it belonged to the army, and they arrest people and probably shoot them for climbing around on their tanks.

I did worry about that for a few minutes, but there was no other way of telling when Nathanial was in his backyard. The fence was solid wood, with no peepholes anywhere. So I had to take my chances on being shot.

When it started getting late, Derek said he had to get home for supper, and I couldn't argue with that one. Getting home for supper is the one major responsibility of every kid who ever lived.

So we went home for supper.

But we met back at the tank right after, and as soon as I climbed to my lookout place, love and excitement squeezed me right around the gizzard.

Nathanial was out there throwing sticks for Phil.

I slid down and grabbed Derek by the collar and hauled him close to the fence. By rolling my eyes, I got the message across.

"Bug off, Derek," I said. "I'm not interested in you. You're too young and boring."

From beyond the fence I could just barely hear Nathanial calling to Phil.

"I love you, Zelda," Derek said in a tiny voice. "You are so beautiful. . . ."

"Louder," I hissed.

"Bug off, Derek," I yelled. "I'm not interested in you. You're too young and boring."

He yelled back at me, "I love you, Zelda. You are so beautiful and wonderful."

"Great," I whispered. "Let's keep going."

"Your hair is too light," I bellowed. "I could never fall in love with a redhead. Only black hair—that's for me. So go away and quit bothering me, Derek."

"But I love you," he yelled back. "You're the most beautiful and wonderful and adorable . . ." He was running down.

"Smart," I hissed.

"And smart," he bellowed back. "I worship and adore you, Zelda. I'll dye my hair black for you."

"But you have blue eyes, Derek," I yelled. "My perfect boyfriend must have deep dark dangerous eyes."

"Okay, I'll dye my eyes, too. Please, Zelda, don't make me go away. Let me be your boyfriend. Please."

He was really getting into this acting stuff. I admired his talent. He was almost convincing me.

"I'm sorry, Derek. I can't love you."

"Oh, please." He was getting tears in his eyes now. "Please, Zelda, you're so beautiful and wonderful and adorable.

And smart. Please let me be your boy-friend."

He grabbed me and kissed me.

"Hey," I whispered, "that wasn't in the script."

"Please let me be your boyfriend."

He was getting tears in his eyes, just like the day I accidentally stepped on his fingers when we were climbing the monkey bars.

I felt sorry for him, so I gave him a hug. That's when he started bawling for real. "Don't make me go away, Zelda," he begged.

I had to take him home. He wouldn't stop crying, and his mother thought I'd stepped on his fingers again.

Oh, well. It was almost dark, and the mosquitoes were getting bad. I went home to wait for morning, when I could find out if Nathanial was getting jealous yet.

I hoped he was. I didn't want to have to go through all that with Derek again.

Especially since he'd forgotten about the eight dollars, and I didn't want to remind him.

❧

The next day was Saturday. It rained all day, and I couldn't think of any way to find out if Nathanial had gotten jealous or not. I lay on the floor watching television, making Mom step over me.

"What's the matter, dumpling?" she asked once.

I felt fat.

"Nothing." I answered through my teeth because my determined chin was in my hand, and I couldn't open my mouth.

How could she let it go at that?

She was supposed to know something was wrong even though I said nothing was. She was supposed to see how sad I was and be extra nice to me till I told her what it was.

Nothing was working for me.

I watched a very old black-and-white

cowboy movie, where the beautiful girl was in love with the cowboy, but all he did was play his guitar and gallop around in clouds of dust. Finally at the end of the movie she got him to kiss her, and all of a sudden he fell in love. I could tell by the music.

I thought about Nathanial.

Maybe if I could get him to kiss me, that would do the trick. It sure worked for the cowboy's girl, and I was as cute as she was.

I rolled over on my back and stuck my feet in the air. I thought and thought, and finally I started grinning. I don't have a determined chin for nothing, I thought.

Nathanial was going to kiss me whether he liked it or not.

ℭ

Mom loves to sleep late on Sunday mornings, so it was no problem for me to get up early and sneak out. I was up on the tank before anyone at Nathanial's house was awake. The tank was all wet with dew, but I was too excited to care.

In my jeans pocket I had a note. I'd written it the night before, on my notepaper with the rainbows across the top. It wasn't all that romantic, but I figured rainbows were better than giraffes, which was what my other notepaper had.

It happened just like I hoped. The back door of Nathanial's house opened, and a man in pants and a pajama top came out, leading Phil the odder hound. He snapped Phil's collar to a chain I'd noticed before, and then he went back in the house. Back to bed, I hoped.

Fast as lightning, I ran through the armory lot, around the corner, around the next corner, and up to Nathanial's driveway.

So far, so good. Nobody had seen me.

I darted up the driveway, hid behind the garage, and eased around it to where Phil could see me.

He barked.

"Shhh, you'll blow it," I whispered. "Come here, nice doggy."

He came up, sort of wagging and bowing to me. I could tell he wasn't going to give me any trouble.

I unsnapped the chain, grabbed Phil's collar, pulled the note out of my pocket, and stuck it in the snap.

Then I ran for it, dragging Phil along with me.

ℰ

The next time I kidnap a dog, I'll remember to take a leash along. Phil was a very big dog. A very big happy dog with a chain collar that was ripping up my hands before I got him to the first corner.

On top of that, Phil was thrilled to be taking me for this wonderful early morning walk. He jumped around and practically jerked my arms out of their sockets.

As we were passing the armory, we

met a big old lady walking a cat on a harness and leash, which is a pretty weird thing to do in the first place.

Phil lunged toward her and pulled me flat, and the cat climbed up the lady.

"Control your animal, young woman," she screeched as she tried to get the cat out of her hairdo. I got my animal under control.

When she was past me she turned and said, "Isn't that the Gorsuch dog?"

"I'm walking him for them," I panted.

"That's nice." She turned and walked away, and I pulled Phil down the Perfect Paradise Trailer Park road.

Dogs weren't allowed in Perfect Paradise.

Maybe no one will notice him, I thought.

I dragged him up the row of trailers to ours and hauled him inside. He was thrilled, especially since the kitchen counter was about eye level for him.

My plan was to hide him in my bedroom, which was at the end of the hall.

The hall was so narrow that when Phil wagged his tail, he whanged both walls. I started dragging him. He dug in his toenails, but the floor was linoleum so he slid all the way.

We were just safely past Mom's bedroom door when she called out in her fuzziest, still-asleep-don't-wake-me-up voice, "Zelda, is that you making all that racket on a Sunday morning?"

Phil heard her voice, twisted out of my hands, and jumped against Mom's door. It burst open.

She screamed. Phil bounded up and landed right in the middle of her bed. He was thrilled.

She wasn't.

"Get in here, Zelda Marie," she yelled.

I knew I was in trouble. I'm Zelda Marie only when things are really bad.

"Where did this come from, and take it right back."

"He followed me home."

"And I'm Martha Washington. Get him off me. Get him out of here."

"I'm keeping him for a friend," I said.

"No. You are not keeping him for a friend or anyone else. You know the no-dogs rule here. Look, if you want a pet this badly we'll get you a gerbil or something nice and tiny like that."

Hmm. A bonus. "Could I get one of those guinea pigs with the long hair that grows in swirls?"

"Maybe. We'll see."

I hate it when she says that.

But before we could settle the matter of the guinea pig, there was a knock on the door. No, more like a pound on the door. A mad pound. With a mad fist.

My note was paying off.

ℭ

Nathanial stood on the little bitty front porch waving my note in his hand. He looked very angry.

Standing below him on our little sidewalk was the man I'd seen putting Phil out. He was standing next to a woman. Nathanial's mother, no doubt. The whole family looked mad enough to chew trucks.

"Give me back my dog!" Nathanial yelled.

My mom came up behind me, holding on to Phil by the collar. She was wearing her nightshirt that looked like a prison uniform with a number across the chest. Her hair was sticking out in funny directions. She didn't look happy about the situation, either.

"This was supposed to be between you and me," I said to Nathanial. "How did all these parents get into it?"

His father said, "Now look here, girl. That dog cost six hundred dollars. He's a valuable purebred with a pedigree as long as your arm, and we want him back right now."

Over the top of my head, Mom said, "How do you do? I'm Ruth Hammersmith. You must be Mr. and Mrs. . . ." She couldn't remember Nathanial's last name. "Won't you come in and have a cup of coffee? I'm sure we can work this out peaceably."

I pinned Nathanial down with my steely eyes and said, "Nathanial and I will settle it out here."

His parents went inside for coffee and left Nathanial and me glaring at each other on the porch.

"You got my note," I said. "You know my terms for returning the hostage."

"Yeah. I have to kiss you."

"Right."

"Wrong."

"Wrong?"

"Right. If I have to kiss you to get my dog back . . . keep the dog."

"Keep the dog!" I wailed. Mrs. Birdsall frowned out her window at me. Our noise was bothering her sinus.

"Keep the dog," he repeated.

"Nathanial, how can you say that? Whatever happened to the great love between a boy and his dog?"

"It's not that great."

"What about all that bragging you were doing about Phil having a pedigree as long as my arm?"

He turned and walked away. "You keep the dog," he said. "I'll keep the pedigree."

I went back inside. What else can you do when the boy you love would rather give away his dog than kiss you?

I found out that Mom and the Gorsuches had already worked out the terms for the return of the kidnapped odder hound.

The terms were: I return Phil.

Mom was very nice about the whole thing, especially after I promised to clean up the mess Phil made wagging his tail across the tabletop and knocking coffee cups and the sugar bowl onto the floor.

She gave me a big long hug that almost smothered me, but it felt good anyway. Then we talked the whole thing over.

She reminded me that kidnapping

was stealing. I hadn't thought about that, and it made me feel rotten. But then she told me several times that there wasn't anything wrong with me. I really was beautiful and wonderful and adorable and her little dumpling, and if Nathanial didn't appreciate me, that was his tough luck.

"It's just because he's not mature enough yet," she explained. "One of these days he'll be ready for a girl-friend, and when he is . . ."

℃

So I'm waiting. I'm sitting here on top of the army tank where I can see his backyard.

And the minute he looks like he's ready . . .

2. Zelda and the Awful F

It was bad enough to be scorned by my true love. But then things got worse. Report Card Day.

Report Card Day is the pits even if you have a regular teacher, but I have Mrs. Green. The other classes at Truman Elementary have nice smiley teachers. We have Mrs. Green.

The other classes have fun stuff on their bulletin boards, Thanksgiving stuff and Valentine's Day stuff. We have alphabets. Do you know how boring it gets, looking at alphabets for a whole year? At Christmas we have red and green alphabets with little piles of snow on top of the letters.

Mrs. Green is twenty feet tall. I've only seen her smile once, and then I wasn't sure it was a smile. The corners of her mouth went back, but then they turned down instead of up.

Kimberley said that's the way Mrs. Green smiles. Kimberley's older brother had Mrs. Green, and he says she smiled once in his class, and that was what it looked like.

Mrs. Green hates kids. The reason she's a teacher is so she can get back at as many kids as possible in her lifetime. Don't ask me why. Her favorite time to get back at us is Report Card Day.

This one was a disaster. I got the worst possible thing you can get.

An F.

I couldn't believe it. I looked down the list: English, B plus. History, C plus. Music, B. Art, A minus. Geography, C. Arithmetic, F.

There it was, glaring up at me.

Arithmetic, F.

I looked at that letter, in blue ink, and it started getting bigger and bigger.

It started flashing like a neon light till you couldn't see the A minus and the B plus at all. Just that one horrible letter.

F.

I wasn't expecting anything wonderful in Arithmetic. I'd been having a lot of trouble since we started fractions. They didn't make sense. When I asked Mrs. Green why "of" meant "times," she glared down at me and said, "Because I say so."

I couldn't take that report card home with an F on it. No mom could possibly love a kid with a F on her record.

I started to panic.

Somehow, I was going to have to get Mom's signature on this thing without her seeing that F.

And the system they've got for report cards is just about foolproof. If you try to write your parent's name on the signing line and pretend you took it home, they can always tell it's not a real signature.

And besides, Mom knows exactly when Report Card Day is. If I didn't bring the crummy thing home, she'd know it right away.

If you lose your report card, they give you a new one. They've got you in a corner, and they know it. The only thing you can do is take it home and get it signed.

I was really scared. I knew I had to do something. The bell was ringing, and Kimberley was waiting by the bus for me, so I had to go.

Kimberley sat with me on the bus. She always sits with me on the bus because we're best friends, but today I wished she would bug off. She gets on my nerves a lot.

The reason we're best friends isn't

because we like each other. It's because we're the only two girls in our class who live at Perfect Paradise Trailer Park, so we have to be best friends.

Kimberley is one of those awful people who is always clean. She never has to comb her hair because it doesn't move. Her face never gets dirty. Her nose never runs. She takes tap dance *and* ballet, and she never lets you forget it.

And of course she would never get an F. She probably wouldn't want a best friend who got an F.

"Let's see your report card," she said as soon as the bus got going.

Kimberley is also the kind who always wants to see other people's report cards and test papers. That's because she always has a better grade than you do, and she wants you to know it.

"I'm not showing you my report card, Kimberley."

"Why not?" she teased. "I bet you got a bad grade. I bet you got a D."

"No, I did not get a D," I said honestly.

"Then why won't you show it to me, Zelda? Are you ashamed of it?"

I felt like punching her. I really felt like hauling off and socking her in the stomach. But I was already in enough trouble. So I decided to use my brains instead.

"Kimberley, I know you're a perfect person and all that, but you have one big fault, in case no one ever told you."

"What?" She said it like she didn't believe me.

"Don't you know it's not polite to ask people to show you their report cards? Didn't anyone ever teach you better manners than that?"

She looked a little steamed. She wasn't used to being criticized—especially by me. I didn't get very many chances. It felt good.

"Look," I explained, "if somebody gets all A's on her report card, and then you come along and ask to see it, she

isn't going to want to hurt your feel-
ings by showing you an all-A report card
when you didn't get one. So that's why
it's not polite to ask. See?"

She looked at me like I was feeding
her a bunch of baloney, which of course
I was. But she couldn't be sure of that,
so she didn't say anything more about
it.

Kimberley and I were the last stop
on the bus, along with Derek. The bus
lets us off on the corner by the armory,
and then we walk up a block and turn
in at the Perfect Paradise road.

Usually I run faster than they do, but
today I had a secret mission. Lose the
report card. I knew I'd get another one
tomorrow, but at least this would give
me time to think.

I walked slower and slower, till Kimberley and Derek were several sidewalk
squares ahead of me. I slipped my hand
into my book bag and pulled out the
report card.

While I was deciding whether to jam

it into the bushes or toss it into the street, I had a better idea. I looked down and saw a sewer grill. Quickly I squatted down and stuffed the report card down the sewer.

"Oops," I said. I stood up and dusted off my knees.

e

Good old Mrs. Birdsall didn't know about Report Card Day, so I was safe till five, when Mom got home. I spent that whole Mrs. Birdsall hour doing my homework. I was trying to make up for the F.

But what I really needed was a way out of the mess.

The first thing Mom said after she got out of her work clothes was "Let's see your report card."

Lots of mothers don't pay that much attention to their kids. Lots of kids are downright neglected. Not me.

Mom was sort of sprawled on the sofa with her shoes off and her belt undone. She was resting up from running her sausage-stuffing machine all day at the packing plant. She had a can of Mountain Dew in her hand and an expectant look on her face.

"Report card?" I asked.

"Report card," she said with a touch of suspicion in her voice.

I looked through my book bag. "Gee, it was in here."

"Is it inside one of your books?"

I picked up each book and shook it. Nothing fell out but a bubble-gum wrapper.

"Maybe you left it at Mrs. Birdsall's," Mom said. "Did you?"

"I don't think so. I'm pretty sure I didn't." I hate it when Mom looks at me with her icy eyes, especially when I'm trying to hide something.

"Well, you'd better find it, Zelda Marie Hammersmith. And you'd better find it fast."

I looked at the floor. "Maybe I lost it on the bus."

She gave me her hardest look and said, "If you lost it, the school office will give you another card. You will bring me a report card by tomorrow, Zelda. Or else."

I hate it when she says "or else." That's the worst threat she can use. She gets to fill in the "or else" later on, when she thinks of something bad enough to do to you. Or else no television for a week. Or else no playing outside after supper. Or else or else or else.

I spent the evening in my room with my homework in front of me, but since I'd already done it at Mrs. Birdsall's, my mind was free to think about my problem.

No later than tomorrow, I'd have to bring home another report card. Mom would have to sign it. And she would read it carefully before she signed it. She always did. And she always remembered the last card.

"C plus in History, Zelda," she'd say. "That's down from a B minus last time.

Better watch it, kid. Better get it back up there."

I could smudge over the F. I could get a drop of water on it so she couldn't tell for sure if it was an F or a B.

No, that wouldn't work. She'd know. Mom could see right through something like that, and if she didn't get me on this end, Mrs. Green would get me on the other end when I took the card back.

Same thing if I tried to match Mrs. Green's blue ink and make the F into a B. They'd know it in a minute.

I'd probably get kicked out of school for that.

I could lose the card again. But they'd go on giving me new ones till next Report Card Day, and they'd get pretty suspicious, besides.

I was lying in bed in the dark, still working on it, when I finally came up with The Plan.

Mom would see the report card tomorrow and sign it and not get mad at me.

Because.

Because she would be so relieved that I didn't get killed when the car ran over me.

ℰ

When I got dressed the next morning, I put on my brown corduroy slacks because they were good for getting dirty in. On top, I wore my undershirt, my pink T-shirt with Miss Piggy on it, and my red plaid blouse over that.

When I packed my book bag, I dropped in my big twenty-four-color box of Crayolas.

The first thing Mrs. Green said after the bell rang was "Pass your report cards forward, please."

She collected them from the front row, counted them, and frowned.

"Two report cards are missing. Who failed to return his or her card?"

She glared around the room like she was accusing us of murder. I raised my hand, and so did Wesley Crookshank. Wesley is the kind who stands up to speak even if he doesn't have to.

He stood up and said, "I'll bring my card tomorrow, Mrs. Green. My daddy was on a business trip last night, and he's the one who signs it."

Mrs. Green nodded. She looked like that was okay with her.

Then she turned her evil eyes on me and said, "Zelda?"

"I lost my card," I muttered.

"Speak up, Zelda. And why are you sitting all hunched over like that?"

I was sitting hunched over because when I looked in the mirror in the girls' room before school started I saw that my pink T-shirt was showing at the neck. I didn't want anybody asking why I was wearing two tops, so I'd been sitting with my shoulders hunched. That way my blouse covered the T-shirt.

I straightened up, put my hands to my throat like I had a frog in there, and said, "I think I lost my card on the bus."

"No you didn't." Mrs. Green narrowed her eyes to little slits. "If the driver had found any report cards on the bus, he would have turned them in at the office. Some children," she said in a heavy voice, "*some* children deliberately try to lose their report cards. Especially if they are ashamed of them."

Kimberley turned around and looked at me like she knew all along I hadn't gotten straight A's.

I didn't say anything. That's usually the best way to handle Mrs. Green. Let her do the talking.

She said, "The office will make out another card for you, Zelda. See that you pick it up before you leave today, and see that you return it, signed, by tomorrow. See that you do that, Zelda."

I cringed down in my seat and nodded.

That afternoon I waited till Kimberley and Derek got off the bus. The first part of The Plan was to get rid of them.

"Why don't you come over to my house?" Kimberley said with an evil look. "We can make doll clothes, or you can show me your report card. . . ."

"Doll clothes," I said in my worst nasty voice. "Who wants to make stupid old doll clothes?"

Derek had disappeared at the first mention of doll clothes. And Kimberley stalked off toward home, walking mad. So I was free.

I had been thinking about The Plan all day, and I had decided on the perfect spot to do it.

There was a hedge of high bushes along the sidewalk in front of the National Guard Armory. And there was a fair amount of traffic on that street. Not too much, because I needed time between cars. But enough so there should be a car or two when I was ready.

ↄ

First came the bruises. I had thought about trying to make blood, but I figured I could never fool anybody with fake blood.

Bruises were different. I crawled back into the bushes and sat down where I couldn't be seen unless someone walked by slowly. I hoped nobody would.

I took my Crayola box out of my book bag and opened it. This box had twenty-four crayons, everything from Burnt Umber to Plum Purple.

I thought for a long time, then pulled out Jade Green, Yellow Gold, Plum Purple, Lavender, Rose Red, and a few others. This part was fun!

I took off my outside blouse, pulled up my T-shirt and undershirt, and then I went to work on my stomach. Green bruises with yellow edges, red-and-purple bruises with green edges, black-and-blue bruises with lavender edges.

It was great! I almost forgot why I was doing it. I did my stomach and my sides and what I could reach of my back. I colored my arms. I pulled up my slacks and pulled down my socks and did my legs.

I thought a while, then pulled off my shoes and socks and did my feet. Different colored bruises on each toe. I tried a few on my face, but it was hard to do where I couldn't see.

Then on to the next step.

I took my blouse and crawled out of the bushes. I looked up and down the street. No cars.

Quickly I laid my blouse in the street. I put it where tires would probably run over it. A nice tire-track print across the blouse would add a lot of believability.

I walked up and down the sidewalk, watching the blouse, watching for cars, watching for anybody I knew who might come along and mess it up at the crucial moment.

My luck held. A car came cruising along, headed right for the blouse. A woman was driving, and the car was full of little kids.

Good, I thought. *She'll be too busy telling them to shut up and sit still to notice the blouse.*

Wrong.

She slammed on her brakes just before her tires got to the blouse. She jumped out, ran around the car, and picked up the blouse. She held it up and looked at it like she was thinking about buying it.

I opened my mouth to say "That's mine," but I couldn't think of any way to explain why I was walking back and forth in front of my own blouse without picking it up myself.

So I didn't say anything. The woman grinned like she'd found money, stuffed my blouse under her sweater, and jumped back into her car and drove away.

Some people are so dishonest! I couldn't believe it!

Well, there was nothing else to do. I looked around to be sure the coast was clear. Then I skinned off my pink Miss Piggy T-shirt, threw it into the street, and dove back into the bushes in just my undershirt.

"Boy," I thought, "if somebody swipes Miss Piggy, I'm in real trouble. Try telling Mrs. Birdsall why I'm coming home in my underwear."

But this time I was in luck. A truck came along, barreled right over Miss Piggy, and left a beautiful tire mark right up the front of it.

Fast as lightning, I jumped out, grabbed the T-shirt, and put it on. Then came the main part of The Plan.

Now or never, I told myself.

I dropped my book bag beside the curb, looked both ways to be sure no one was watching, and then I lay down, sort of half in the street and half on the curb.

It was the worst uncomfortable-ness you can imagine. I wiggled around till my head was at least comfortable on the grass by the curb. I flung one arm out dramatically, got one leg sort of crooked looking, and closed my eyes.

I wished then that I'd tried fake blood. It would have made the picture perfect.

℃

Brakes screeched.

Car doors slammed.

Somebody screamed.

I concentrated on keeping my eyes shut and my face straight.

"Oh, my God, she's dead," a man's voice said.

Someone screamed again.

Someone else said, "I'll call an ambulance. Don't touch her. Don't move her."

An ambulance. I hadn't counted on that. I fluttered my eyes open and said in a weak voice, "I'm not dead."

"She's not dead," somebody called out.

"It must have been a hit-and-run," the man said close to my ear. "Somebody better call the police."

"No, that's okay," I said, struggling to sit up. The man pushed me back down.

"Don't move, honey. The ambulance is coming. Don't move."

He sounded so shaken that I suddenly felt sorry to be doing this to him. All I'd figured on was someone stopping and taking me home and calling Mom at work to tell her I'd had an accident but I was okay.

"I'm not hurt," I said again and tried to sit up.

The man was still leaning over me, and a woman was behind him. The woman said, "Don't let her move, Harold. She probably has a concussion. And look at her skin. Look how . . . green? Look how green it is. And purple. And all those other colors. She's bleeding internally."

I started feeling sick and faint then, thinking about bleeding internally.

There was a siren, louder and louder.

"I don't need an ambulance. Don't take me to the hospital," I said in my healthiest voice.

Another siren joined in, and all of a sudden I was surrounded by men in police uniforms and other men in ambulance uniforms. They slid me onto a stretcher and shoveled me into the back end of the ambulance.

I heard a policeman saying, "Did anyone here see the accident? Can anyone describe the car? License number?"

The ambulance doors closed and the sirens went on again, and we tore away.

Nothing was going the way it was supposed to.

They wheeled me into the hospital,

and before I could sit up and say, "Hey, I recovered," I was surrounded by nurses and doctors. They poked at me and rolled my eyelids back and wrapped a rubber-bag thing around my arm and pumped it so full of air that my arm almost choked.

It was more attention than I'd ever had in my life. It would have been great if it weren't for the fact that I was on the edge of very big trouble.

"This discolored skin, doctor," one of the nurses said. She rubbed her thumb over my arm and then frowned down at her thumb.

It was purply green.

I sank back and closed my eyes.

Another nurse said in a low voice, "Look at her little shirt. The car must have passed directly up her body and over her face. A miracle . . ."

I opened one eye and saw the doctor rubbing his thumb over the nurse's green-and-purple thumb.

I closed my eye quickly.

My mind was running around like a hamster on a wheel, trying to find a story that would get me out of this. There wasn't any.

"Can you sit up, Zelda?" the doctor asked me, with a kind of frown in his voice. I figured they got my name from my book bag. They probably had already called Mom at work.

The worst was yet to come.

I sat up, opened my eyes, and faced the music.

Standing just behind the doctor was a policeman. He looked familiar. He'd been at the scene of the non-accident. I wanted to play dead some more, but that policeman scared me.

He came forward, bent down over me, and said, "Now, honey, just try to remember. What did the car look like? What color was it?"

Some other guy in a green outfit came through the curtain and said, "Doctor, they're ready for her in X-ray now. Shall I take her along?"

"No," I said. "I don't need an x-ray."

"Honey," the policeman said, "you didn't happen to see the license plate, did you? Was it a Kansas plate?"

I stared at him. How did he think I was going to have time to look at license plates while I was being run over?

The doctor's face poked down in front of mine again, and he held up two fingers. "How many fingers do you see?" he asked me.

"Four, and a thumb," I said.

"Double vision," he murmured.

What I meant was I saw four fingers, two sticking up and two folded over, but he didn't give me time.

Somebody pulled up my shirt, and they found my stomach artwork. The policeman turned pale, the doctor frowned . . . but the nurse rubbed my stomach and got another colorful thumb. Violet and blue and yellow this time.

I figured the jig was up.

I figured it was the end of the world, and it couldn't get any worse.

That was when the curtain opened again, and Mom came in.

ℭ

Right away when I saw her face I realized what an awful thing I had done. More awful than getting the F in the first place.

Mom looked scared out of her mind.

"I'm okay, Mom."

She grabbed me and hugged me till I had to fight my way up for air.

"My baby, my dumpling," she said over and over.

Finally the doctor said, "Mrs. Hammersmith, I believe there's been a hoax here."

I didn't know what a hoax was, but I had a terrible feeling I was guilty of it.

"Hoax?" Mom said. "You mean . . . a hoax? You mean . . ." She grabbed me by the shoulders and stared at me.

She can have icy eyes even when they're red from crying.

"I'm sorry, Mom," I wailed. I tried to throw myself against her, but she was holding me out where she could look at me. She stared at the tire track up Miss Piggy.

She stared at the crayon bruises on my face. I was crying seriously now, so the bruises were probably running a little bit.

"You mean," she said in her you're-really-in-for-it-now voice, "that you were not run over by a car?"

I shook my head. "I'm sorry I wasn't," I wailed.

"When I get you home, you're going to wish you had been, Zelda Marie Hammersmith."

The policeman growled something about false accident reports being against the law.

The doctor gave me a cold look and told Mom to see the woman at the desk about the charges for the ambulance and the emergency care.

One nurse went away shaking her head. The other one kind of winked at me like she was wishing me luck with all the trouble ahead.

It was going to take more than a wink to get me through *this.*

In the car on the way home, I tried not to talk at all. I tried to shrink and disappear, but that never does work.

Mom gave me a dark look. "The bruises?" she asked.

"Crayons," I muttered.

We drove on in silence.

"The tire tracks on your T-shirt?" she thundered.

"I took it off and threw it in the street," I whispered.

She didn't remember I'd worn the red plaid blouse this morning. I didn't remind her, either.

I glanced up at her once, and I thought I saw one corner of her mouth twitching like it was trying to smile and she wouldn't let it. But I decided it couldn't have been a smile. It must have been fury.

It wasn't till we were home and I was in the bathtub un-bruising myself that she got down to the bottom line.

"Why, Zelda? Why did you feel you had to give your mother a heart attack at work and take twenty years off her life?"

I never have figured out what she means when she says "took twenty years off my life," or ten years or whatever. You'd think she'd want to be younger.

But this was no time for deep thoughts. Mom was waiting for an answer. She was sitting on the toilet lid, which is the only place to sit in our bathroom, frowning down at me while I scrubbed the colors off my leg.

"Why, Zelda?"

I sighed and gave up.

"Because I got an F in arithmetic."

"*What?*"

I pulled in a long breath and said, "I

got an F on my report card, and I was scared to show it to you."

"So you threw yourself in front of traffic?"

I stood up, and she wrapped a towel around me and started helping me dry, like she used to when I was little.

"I didn't throw myself in front of traffic—only my T-shirt," I explained. "I just lay down by the curb. I was careful to stay out of the way of cars."

She took me by the shoulders again, but this time she sounded softer.

"But why, dumpling? Why were you so scared? Did you think I'd hit you, or what?"

I shook my head. "I figured you wouldn't love me anymore," I whispered.

We hugged each other a lot then, and she told me I was her child and she would always love me, no matter what incredibly stupid things I did.

"Even if I get F's on my report card?"

"You'd better not, ever again," she growled.

℄

So here I am, spending one week of evenings in my room doing arithmetic. No television, no playing outside after supper.

Mom said she'd help me with fractions. But when I asked her why "of" means "times," she said she'd never figured that one out herself.

"You'll just have to take Mrs. Green's word for it," she said.

I know one thing for sure. I'm never going to get an F again. Or if I do, I'm not going to try to hide it. Or if I do try to hide it, I won't try faking another car accident. Or if I do fake another car accident, I'll find something better than crayons for the bruises.

8. Zelda and the Mean Guy

've been having some other trouble, too.

His name is Gerald.

He's been giving me trouble ever since first grade, when he gave the whole class pinkeye. Three times.

And laughed about it.

Gerald is smaller than I am, but he makes up for it with extra meanness. He's got short, chopped-off hair that sticks out in funny places, and little red eyes. And his favorite hobby is picking his nose.

His other favorite hobby is doing mean things.

He can stick his foot out to trip people faster than the eye can see. Even Mrs. Green has never actually seen his foot in the aisle, and she sees everything.

She can see a note being passed while she's writing on the blackboard with her back to us. She can see a tongue being stuck out, way in the back row, while she's reading to us.

She can see a comic book clear down in a person's lap while she's still standing in the hall talking to another teacher before the bell rings!

Yet she has never once seen Gerald's foot actually in the aisle when someone trips over it.

In winter you don't ever want to get near him outside when he's got one hand behind his back. He'll mash snow in your face or down the back of your neck, quicker than lightning.

And everybody who knows anything at all stays away from him in the swimming pool. You'll get a nose full of water every time, if you don't. He'll grab your ankles underwater and pull you down just for the fun of it.

But the very worst thing is Gerald's arm burns. Arm burns are his specialty. If they ever have arm burns in the Olympics, Gerald is our man.

An arm burn is when somebody puts two hands around your arm, close together, and then twists them in opposite directions. It feels like your skin is ripping off, and you get a big red mark around your arm.

The other day during library period, Gerald came up to me all happy and friendly. He didn't even have his finger up his nose. He looked almost human, standing there smiling.

He said, "Hey, Zelda, I've got something for you. Come over here behind the castle."

Our library has a lot of good stuff in it, like a bathtub full of pillows that you can climb in, to read. And it's got mobiles hanging all over the place that the sixth-grade kids make in Art. And a cardboard hand-puppet theater in the shape of a big castle.

Gerald wanted me to go behind the castle with him. Of course I knew better. But I'd already checked my books out, and it wasn't quite time for the bell to ring.

"I don't trust you," I told him.

"It's not a trick. Honest, Zelda. I've got a present for you, but it's a secret. You have to come over here to get it."

I gave him a black look. "You're going to get me over there and give me an arm burn, Gerald. I know you."

"No, I'm not. Honest. Cross my heart and hope to die, stick a needle in my eye."

Well, that's a pretty strong oath. I wavered. I didn't think even Gerald would take the chance of breaking that oath and getting a needle in his eye.

I gave him another suspicious look and took a couple of steps toward the castle.

He jumped behind it and fished

something out of his pocket. I couldn't see what. He kept his fist closed.

I took another step closer.

"What is it?" I said suspiciously.

"Something really good." He peeked into his fist and smiled. "You'll really like this, Zelda."

It was possible that even Gerald could do something nice. Anything was possible. And I love presents.

I took the final step behind the castle and tried to see what was in his fist.

"Here's your present," he said. "A nice red bracelet."

And quick as a snake striking, he grabbed my arm and gave me a burn.

I yelled.

Of course I know you're not supposed to yell in a library. Everybody knows that. But I couldn't help myself. It was the worst arm burn I'd ever gotten. And I was so mad at him for tricking me that I couldn't stand it.

Mrs. Green was on top of us before my yell quit echoing.

"What are you two doing back here

in the corner? And shouting! I'm ashamed of you both."

She marched us back to our room, and we had to stay in from recess for the rest of the week. One thing is always true about Mrs. Green: If there's any trouble, she punishes everyone involved, even if you only happened to be passing by at the time. Even if somebody is passing you a note, and you don't even want them to do it, you still get punished right along with the person who passed it.

And yelling behind the castle is worse than passing notes.

Three whole days of not going out for recess. I didn't think I could stand it. I have to run every once in a while, or my legs start falling asleep. If I sit too long, my fanny starts aching. My back gets stiff.

I hate having to stay in at recess! I started hating Gerald more than I'd ever hated him before.

Kimberley came over after supper.

Mom and I were doing the dishes

when Kimberley got there. I'd already told Mom about Gerald and the brace-let he gave me behind the castle.

When Kimberley got there I told it again for her and made a little more of a story out of it.

"Somebody should do something about that little bully," Mom said, turning on the television and sinking down into the beanbag chair in front of it.

I could tell she wanted to watch her program, so Kimberley and I went into my room for a meeting on my bed.

"I want to get even with that Gerald once and for all," I snarled through gritted teeth.

"How?" Kimberley made herself comfortable on my pillow, then turned her attention to me.

"I don't know *how*. That's why we're having this meeting. What could we do to him that would stop him? And that wouldn't get us into trouble?"

"What do you mean, we? This is

your big idea. You're the one who got into trouble for yelling in the library."

That's the kind of friend Kimberley is.

"I'd like to teach him. Get back at him. Make him quit picking on everybody," I muttered. "Maybe scare him good."

"How?"

"I don't know. Make him think I was a ghost or something, maybe."

"You mean like in *A Christmas Carol?* Where mean old Scrooge got turned into a nice guy after all those ghosts scared him?"

"Yeah. . . ." My face lit up. I hadn't been thinking about Scrooge until she said it, but I decided to take credit for the idea anyway.

And in fact, maybe that had been where I got the idea. It was getting close to Christmas, and that old movie had been on television a few nights before. Mom had watched it. I was reading, but I probably heard some of it and didn't even know it.

Suddenly my Big Plan began to hatch.

ↄ

Since Mrs. Green didn't want to give up her recesses to watch Gerald and me, she sent us to the library. Back to the scene of the crime.

I wondered what teachers did for fun during recess. They couldn't run around the playground and get the buzzies out of their legs. I figured they went someplace of their own and smoked cigarettes or talked about each other, or whatever teachers do for fun.

It must be awful to be so old that you can't run around a playground at recess. Of course, it was even worse to be a *kid* who couldn't run around the playground at recess. The library was nice, but it wasn't the same as running around.

The next day, I got in the bathtub in the library and squirmed down into the pillows and stuck a book up in front of me so everybody would think I was reading.

Then I thought.

I'd been working on my Plan ever since last night, but it had some pretty big problems. Where was I going to do this ghost act to scare Gerald? I mean, if it's going to be scary, it has to be at night. And the only place Gerald went at night was his own bed.

I knew where he lived. It was only a couple of blocks from Perfect Paradise. I'd seen it from the bus window.

But if I carried out the Plan at his house, how was I going to get in? And how was I going to get out on my own, that late at night?

The other problem was the ghost itself. I figured if I just dressed up in a sheet and tried to scare him, he would see right away that I was just a kid under a sheet. You see them all over the place at Halloween.

No, a ghost should be something floating around in the air. It should look kind of drifty and bodyless.

While I was working on that problem, the bell rang, and I had to get out of the bathtub. I had put my book away and started out the door when I noticed the clown.

He'd been there for weeks, but I just hadn't looked at him lately. He was made of cardboard—a life-sized clown with a silly grin on his face and one hand held up.

In that hand was the answer to my problem. In that hand he held a bunch of balloons. They were big ones, the kind filled with that special gas that makes them stay up in the air better than regular balloons.

A balloon like that, I figured, with something draped over it . . .

I ran back to my classroom, grinning.

᳂

The next recess I asked the librarian if I could have one of the balloons, and she said no. It would spoil the display, and it wouldn't be as nice for all the children to enjoy, and I didn't want to be selfish, did I?

Yes, I did.

Actually I didn't think I was being selfish. I figured that getting Gerald to stop giving everybody arm burns wasn't selfish. It would do the school more good than having six balloons in the clown's hand instead of five.

But you can't argue with a librarian. She was nicer than Mrs. Green, but I could tell she thought I just wanted the balloon for myself.

So I had to settle for asking her where I could buy that kind of balloon with the special gas in it. She told me about Ace Novelty and Display Store on Western Avenue.

The next day was Saturday. I asked Mom if I could spend a little of my Christmas money early.

"You haven't gotten it yet," she said. I hate it when she is so logical.

"I know I haven't gotten it yet, but Gramma Humphrey always gives me ten dollars, so I know I'm going to get it, so

why can't I spend a little bit now?
There's something I really need to buy.
Now."

There is a point where begging mys-
teriously turns into whining. Begging
a little bit is allowed. Begging too much
is ignored.

Whining is punished.

So I was trying very hard not to get
over the border into whining. But the
balloon was so important that I had to
keep up the begging.

Maybe Mom was getting some
Christmas spirit or something, because finally, after lunch, she said,
"What is this that you can't live without?"

"A balloon with special gas in it. You
can get them at Ace Novelty Store on
Western Avenue."

She gave me a look, with one eye-
brow higher than the other.

Then she said, "Okay, okay, I give
up. I have to go to the mall this afternoon. We can stop at your balloon place
on the way."

I gave her a big bear hug. The Plan was underway.

ↄ

The next part of The Plan was going to be tough. I was going to have to pretend to like Gerald.

I went over to his house Sunday afternoon. It had snowed the night before, so it wasn't hard to get out by telling Mom I wanted to build a snow fort in the picnic area at the back of the trailer park.

I started back there, then I cut through the parking lot behind the armory and ran down to Gerald's street.

In Gerald's neighborhood the yards all sloped downhill from the street. You could drive down the driveway, around the corner of the house, and into the garage in the basement of the house.

I looked to make sure Gerald's house was that way, too. It was.

Good, I thought.

Then I got all my courage up and rang the front doorbell.

His mother answered.

"Can Gerald come out and play with me?" I asked.

"Who are you?"

I was pretty well wrapped up with scarves and caps and hoods, so she had to bend over to try to see my face.

"Zelda Hammersmith," I said. "I live over there."

She got tired of standing in the cold and told me to come in.

"Gerald," she bellowed. "You've got a friend here to see you."

He came out from the hall, looking surprised. He probably figured he didn't have any friends.

"You want to come out and build a snow fort or something?" I asked him.

He was too surprised to answer.

His mother said, "I don't think I want you out in this weather, Gerald. You'll get a runny nose. Why don't you children play inside? Gerald, show Zelda your new dragon game, why don't you?"

That was fine with me. I didn't want to play outside anyhow. I was just here to get the lay of the land, as they say.

Gerald's mother unwound me from my scarf and pulled off my boots and stuck my mittens in my jacket pockets where I wouldn't forget them.

Then I followed Gerald into his room. *If my friends could see me now,* I thought.

I memorized the house as I went. I saw where the stairs came up from the basement, and where Gerald turned at the end of the hall and opened the door to . . . his room.

I stood in the doorway and stared.

At my house, every Saturday morning is clean-your-room time. No matter what other important things I might have to do that morning, clean-your-room-time comes first.

My room is mostly just my bed, with a little walking-around space on two sides, and a dresser and the closet. Gerald's room was another world.

It was lots bigger than my room, for one thing. For another thing, the floor was invisible.

It was carpeted with toys. Also clothes and junk. There were toy shelves around two walls, but they were empty. Everything that had ever been invented was on that floor.

I took a quick look at the bed. I had planned to sneak in here at night and hide under his bed. Then I could float the ghost balloon around near the ceiling, and start talking and wake him up.

It wasn't going to work, though. Gerald had a waterbed. There was no underneath to it. Still, a room like this must have a good hiding place. In the corners, clothes were piled halfway up the walls.

I was trying to find a clear place on the floor for my feet when something on the bed moved.

It was a dog.

"That's Fang," Gerald said. "He

doesn't like strangers, so you'd better watch it around him."

The dog raised his head and looked at me, then went back to sleep. I couldn't tell what kind of dog he was—something on the order of a collie, I decided. He was fat, and his nose had lots of gray hairs on it, so I figured he must be very old. He probably didn't even have any fangs left. I hoped.

Gerald was still looking at me like he couldn't figure out what I was doing there. I couldn't blame him. But finally he turned on the television set that was half-buried behind a life-sized bear in the form of a chair.

He plugged in a video game about dragons chasing each other in and out of caves. We played for a while, but I always had to let him beat me or he'd start grabbing at my arm. I was wearing long sleeves, so that helped, but I still didn't trust him.

I didn't stay any longer than I had to. I'd gotten the information I needed.

Fang slept through my whole visit.

ℰ

I stopped at Kimberley's on my way home to fix up her end of the story.

She said I could come for a sleepover that night, but I shouldn't come till later because they were eating supper at her aunt's house.

I told Mom I was going to Kimberley's. I had my long white nightgown in a paper bag, along with my toothbrush and comb. I carried the balloon in my other hand.

Mom didn't worry that I was going alone since Kimberley lived just three trailers away.

I was in luck. Nobody was home yet at Kimberley's. I ran past, took the shortcut through the armory lot, and headed for Gerald's house.

Next, I had to see if Gerald's garage door was still unlocked. If they had already locked up for the night, I was in big trouble.

I sneaked around the corner of the

house, down the driveway, to the door beside the big roll-up garage door.

The little door was unlocked!

I eased it open and edged in.

When I could finally see a little in the dark, I looked around. Right there in front of me were the stairs going up to the hall beside the kitchen. I remembered that part of the house.

Upstairs, I could hear a television going, and voices, and some music. Good. Plenty of noise up there.

I squinched myself between the wall and the washing machine and tried to get comfortable. It was going to be a good long wait before everybody was in bed.

ℰ

Sitting on that cold hard floor was uncomfortable—and it was boring! Boring, boring, boring.

I practiced the speech I was going to give Gerald.

My hand went to sleep, and my balloon got away from me and bounced up against the ceiling. I had to wave my hand back and forth in the air for five minutes before I found the balloon string and got it back under control.

After the longest time in the world, the basement door opened right above my head.

I held my breath.

Gerald's father came tromping down, down, down the stairs, almost on top of me.

I tried to think what I'd say when he found me hiding by his washing machine. There was no good excuse for being here. None at all.

He turned the lock on the outside door that I'd come through. Then he yawned, scratched himself on the stomach, and climbed slowly back up the stairs again.

After that the house got quieter, but there was still something playing up there, a television or a radio or something.

My seat fell asleep.

I worried about how late it was getting. If it got too late, Kimberley's mother might call my mom to check on me, and then I'd be in real trouble.

Finally it got all quiet upstairs.

I took my nightgown out of the sack, stuffed the balloon inside it, and started up the stairs.

There was just enough light to see the edges of things.

At the top, I opened the door a crack and listened. I couldn't hear anything. With the balloon under my elbow, I tiptoed down the hall to Gerald's room.

I opened the door.

It was pretty dark in there. I could barely see the outline of him. He was lying on his side, sleeping. It looked like his back was to me. Good.

He was breathing awfully loud. In fact, he was snoring. That's probably what happens to people who go around with their fingers up their noses all the time.

I had to slide my feet along the floor because if I lifted my foot, it was bound to come down on a toy.

Over in the far corner was the best place, I figured. I got behind the bear chair and pulled a heap of jeans and socks and sweaters around me till I was almost invisible.

Then came the big moment.

I started letting the balloon's string out a little bit at a time. Gradually the balloon started to float toward the ceiling, my nightgown hanging from it.

It was a wonderful sight!

It was right next to a hot air register that was close to the ceiling. The air blowing out from the register made the nightgown move around. Its arms wafted out. Its hem danced in the draft.

It looked exactly like a ghost. It would have scared the socks off me if I hadn't known what it was. It about half scared me anyhow.

Okay, I told myself. *Here goes.*

I hummed a little bit—not a song,

just a humming sound to get Gerald awake.

He moved around and kind of snorted.

"Gerald," I croaked in my deepest voice. "Gerald, wake up and face the music."

I couldn't tell if he was awake, so I kept going.

"I am the ghost of George Washington," I said. "I have come back to haunt you for hurting people at school. That's not nice, Gerald."

I waited. He didn't say anything. He was probably too scared.

"You are an evil person, Gerald. You must change your ways, and quit picking on other kids, especially Zelda Hammersmith, Gerald. . . ."

I drew out my voice like a ghost would sound.

Still nothing but snorts and snuffles from the bed.

I decided I'd have to talk louder.

"I am the ghost of George Washington, Gerald. I have come to haunt you until you quit giving arm burns to kids. You must never give arm burns any- more, Gerald, especially to Zelda Ham- mersmith. Do you hear me, Gerald?"

I got louder toward the end.

Suddenly Gerald came up off the bed, barking and attacking the night- gown.

A gunshot went off.

The nightgown fell dead.

The bedroom light came on, and I wished I could fall dead, too.

◌

I blinked in the light.

Gerald's mother and father stood in the door, staring at me. I turned and looked around the room.

Gerald wasn't there.

But Fang was. He was snarling and tearing my nightgown to shreds. He had already bitten the balloon and exploded it.

"What on earth?" Gerald's father said.

"Zelda?" his mother said. "What in the world . . ."

"Where is Gerald?" I asked. If I asked them questions, maybe they'd forget to ask me what I was doing there.

Fat chance.

"Never mind where Gerald is," his mother said, getting pretty red in the face. "Explain yourself, young lady."

I figured I'd better explain myself. There wasn't any other way out of it.

"Gerald was supposed to be here," I said. "I was just going to scare him a little bit, so he'd quit giving us arm burns."

"Arm burns?"

"What's your phone number? I'm calling your mother."

"What does she mean, arm burns?"

The two of them were talking so hard at each other that I was hoping I could sort of ease past them, but they got me.

Gerald's father called Mom, and before he hardly had a chance to hang up, she was there.

I stood halfway behind Mom; she held on to me, either protecting me from them or not letting me escape—I wasn't sure which.

Gerald's parents told Mom their side of it, about how I was guilty of breaking and entering. They told her I had tried to give their poor little baby boy a heart attack—except that he was spending the night at his cousin's.

Then good old Mom took me by the shoulders and said, "All right, Zelda. Let's hear your side of it."

So I told about the arm burns and the tripping and the time he poked a pencil into Trudy Wall's ear and almost punctured her eardrum. I knew I was tattling. I knew it was almost as bad to tattle as to do the things that were being tattled about. But I couldn't help it. I got started, and it just kept coming out.

Then of course I began to cry. I didn't want to, but it was like when you fall down and scrape all the skin off your elbow and act very brave about it. But when you get home, your mom says, "Oh, poor baby, what did you do to your elbow? Come here and let me fix it up for you." And *then* you cry.

Well, I had a good bawl against Mom's stomach, and Mom apologized to them because I'd broken in, and then they said they'd have a talk with Gerald about the arm burns.

Mom and I walked home on the snowy sidewalk, holding hands. I was snuffling, and I could tell she was trying not to smile.

"I'd better call Kimberley and tell her I'm not coming over," I said.

Mom said, "I already called."

I sniffled. "Am I in trouble?"

I looked up at her quickly, and saw her snuffing out a grin that she didn't want me to see.

"I can't exactly approve of your tactics here, Zelda Marie."

"I know it." I drooped my head.

"On the other hand," she said, "you tried to handle a bad situation, and you used imagination and courage to do it. Bullies are a problem. We had one in my school when I was your age."

"What did you do about him?" I asked.

"Nothing. Just tried to stay out of his way, and after a while he moved to Chicago."

She put her hand on top of my head.

"You could have told me about Gerald," she said. "I could have taken up the matter with his parents or with Mrs. Green."

I shrugged.

"Well," she said as we turned in our road and headed for our trailer, "I think you've probably learned your lesson on this one, don't you?"

I nodded as hard as I could.

"I don't think you're likely to do any more wandering when you tell me you're going to Kimberley's, are you?"

I shook my head as hard as I could.

"Okay, then, we'll let it go at that."

Now, every time Gerald sees me, he shoots me nasty looks. But at least he has not given one single arm burn to anybody.

Now he pinches.

4. Zelda and the Really Great Gift

It was November 1, and in case you don't know what that means, it means only eight more shopping days till Mom's birthday.

Last year Mom slipped Mrs. Birdsall five dollars, and Mrs. Birdsall took me to Wal-Mart and helped me pick out a pair of earrings on a piece of cardboard. Mom acted thrilled and told me that if she ever got her ears pierced, my earrings would be the first ones she'd wear.

The years before that, I don't even

remember her birthday, so I must have been too little.

But this year I made up my mind to give Mom the best birthday present she ever had. This year I was old enough to pick out the present myself and use my own money. I had seventeen dollars in my quarter bank, and I figured that would be enough to buy her a really great present, if I could just figure out *what.*

From what I could remember of last year, Mom's birthdays aren't very exciting. Her friends at work take her out to lunch at Pizza Hut and give her silly presents, like a long poem written on toilet paper, or a *Playgirl* magazine with black tape over all the dirty pictures.

My dad always sends her an autographed picture of himself playing a guitar, just like he was already a Nashville star. One picture even had a beautiful lady singer standing with her arm around him. That didn't seem like a very good present to be sending Mom. She didn't think so, either. She set a frozen rump roast on the picture, and by the time the meat had thawed, Daddy and the lady singer had melted into a pulpy, soggy mess.

On my birthdays, Mom always takes the day off from work and takes me and as many friends as I ask to Holiday Park or Fun-O-Rama or wherever I want. And she always gives me just what I want most, as long as it doesn't cost very much. Last year it was a rock-star doll with green hair and metal clothes.

So I really wanted to give her a birthday she'd never forget, partly because she never had very good birthdays, and partly because she always gave me such good ones.

The big problem was finding out what she really wanted that didn't cost more than seventeen dollars' worth of quarters. I didn't want to ask her, because then it wouldn't be a surprise. I was going to have to be subtle and crafty, and sneak up on her.

I tried listening hard every time she talked to one of her friends on the phone, but the subject of birthday presents never came up.

I got Mrs. Birdsall to talk to Mom and try to find out, but that didn't work, either. She said that Mom didn't want to talk about birthdays. Mom told her this one was Number Thirty-nine, and she just wasn't going to have any more after this one. I don't understand that attitude. Thirty-nine is already so old. Why would anyone even worry about it after that? And who would not want to have birthdays, even if all you got was a poem on toilet paper?

Finally I made a direct approach, in my subtle way. "Mom," I said one night while we were washing dishes, "what was the best birthday present you ever got?"

"German measles," she said.

"What?"

"German measles. A little neighbor boy came to my party and infected everyone, which was most of the third grade. I had to miss a dentist appointment, and by the time I was out of quarantine, the tooth had come out without having to be pulled."

"Oh," I said, understanding. "But what was the best present you ever had when you got old?"

She shot me a dirty look. "I haven't gotten old yet, and I don't intend to. Thirty-nine is not old. I'm just approaching my prime."

I decided to ignore that silliness. Everyone knows your prime is around thirteen. I said, "Seriously, Mom, didn't Daddy give you nice presents when you were first in love?"

"Oh." She shrugged and started wiping off the counter. "He gave me things when he had to. Perfume, which I never wear. A nightgown once, but I

always liked pajamas better. Nightgowns get all wrapped around me till I
can't move."

Cross off perfume and nightgowns,
I thought.

I decided to try a different angle.
"What was the one thing you always
wanted and never got?"

She stopped wiping and leaned
against the counter, looking like she
was miles away. "A pony. Of course. I
was a normal American girl. I ate my
heart out for a pony the whole time I
was growing up."

Aha, I thought. *Now we're getting
somewhere.*

☾

Perfect Paradise had a rule against
dogs, but they never said that we
couldn't have a horse.

I spent Saturday cleaning out the
storage shed. Every lot in our trailer
park has a metal storage shed at the

back. Our shed is gray with green trim, and over the door is a little black plastic eagle.

Our shed is three arm-stretches wide and five arm-stretches long. Just about the right size for a horse to live in, I figured. Of course there were no windows, so I wasn't sure what he was going to do for air. And he'd have to keep his head down. But still, how many horses get a black plastic eagle over their door?

I used my wagon to haul bags and boxes of junk to the big metal dumpster behind the National Guard Armory. I found a trap door in the skirting around the bottom of our trailer and rolled the lawn mower under there. The stepladder went under the trailer, too, along with everything else that used to be in the shed.

When Zelda Hammersmith cleans out a shed, it is *cleaned out.*

Mom thought I was wonderful for doing all that cleaning. I was scared she'd get suspicious of why I was doing it, but she didn't. She didn't have any idea that her greatest childhood wish was about to come true.

Sunday morning was my big chance. I opened the fat Sunday paper, spread it out on the floor, went right past the funnies, and began wading through the Want Ads. There were pages and pages of jobs and apartments and used cars, but finally I found the column that said, "Horses, Ponies."

I had already decided Mom was too big for a pony, so I just looked at horse ads. The first thing I saw was prices. They were awful. Five hundred dollars. Two thousand dollars. Awful! The lowest one I found was one hundred, and that was for a baby horse, too young to ride.

Some of the ads didn't give prices. They were the ones that talked about lots of horses instead of just one for sale. I decided those ads would be my best bet.

I listened outside Mom's bedroom door to be sure she was still sound asleep. Then I pulled the phone as far around the corner as it would go and called one of the ads.

A lady answered. "Do you have any horses for around seventeen dollars?" I asked her.

She laughed and hung up.

My determined chin got more determined, and I tried another one. A man answered.

"Do you have any horses for around seventeen dollars? Maybe a small one?"

"What are you, a kid or something?" he snarled, and hung up.

This was going to take some more planning.

I ate a bowl of cereal and a peach and thought about it.

I knew that if this were a story on television, there would be a happy ending. Some grown-up would take a liking to the kid and say, "How much money do you have? That's exactly how much this horse costs." He'd do it to be nice, of course, because he could see that the cute little kid was trying to do a beautiful, unselfish thing.

So why wasn't it working for me? I was a cute little kid—I was trying to buy a horse to make my mom's dream come true. Why did people hang up on me?

I decided my approach needed a little fixing up.

The next ad said, "Horses, ponies, all types, well-broke, priced to sell."

I got into cute-kid position, pulled in my determined chin, and twinkled my eyes. I got my soft voice ready and dialed.

"Yeah?" a man growled.

I hung on to my sweetness and said, "Hello, I'm a little girl, and I want to buy my mom a horse for her birthday. I don't have very much money. We live on welfare, and, see, my mom is crippled. She's supposed to ride a horse every day, to exercise her poor crippled legs, and we can't afford to rent one at the stables, so I was wondering if you might have a very cheap horse that you could sell me? See, I love my mother very much, and I want her to get out of the wheelchair and dance again."

My voice broke a little at the end, and I had real tears coming out of my eyes, thinking about my mother in her wheelchair never dancing again.

The man didn't say anything. I had the feeling he was trying to figure out if I was for real.

"Are you for real?" he growled.

"Of course!"

"You're really a little kid trying to buy a horse for your crippled mother?"

"I really am a little kid," I assured him.

He thought for a while more. Then he said, "How much money you got?"

It was working. Just like on television. I'd tell him how much, and he'd say that was exactly how much the horse cost.

"Seventeen dollars," I told him, breathless with excitement.

"That's exactly how much old Biscuit costs," he said, right on cue. I almost yelled hooray in his ear, but just in time I remembered to be sweet. We made the deal, I gave him our address, and he promised to deliver Biscuit at four o'clock on Friday afternoon.

I could hardly wait.

ℰ

I could barely keep a straight face around Mom all that week. This was going to be the best birthday she ever had. And we were going to have a horse! I figured I could make enough money selling rides on him to pay for his hay and oats. And this was definitely going to make me the most popular kid in this whole part of town.

I let Kimberley in on the secret and

made her spit in her hand and shake on it that she wouldn't tell anyone. I knew she'd keep that swear because she hates to spit in her hand.

We asked her mother for an old sheet to use in a special secret project, and she gave us one. What I really wanted was a huge red satin bow to tie around Biscuit's neck for gift wrapping, but the sheet was as close as I could come without spending any money.

Kimberley and I cut the sheet into big wide strips, and her mother sewed the ends together to make one gigantic ribbon. If it had been red it would have been perfect, but this was the only old sheet available. It was white, with bunches of yellow-and-purple flowers.

Next, we asked Kimberley's mom for a big piece of white cardboard. I wanted to make a gigantic gift tag and write "Happy Birthday, Mom" on it. But the only white cardboard in their whole house was the lid of a shoe box.

I took a red Magic Marker and wrote

"H. B. M." on it. I figured Mom would know what that meant when we all yelled "Happy Birthday!"

When we got up on Friday morning I didn't wish Mom happy birthday. I pretended I didn't even know it was her birthday. That would make the surprise even better.

All day at school I could hardly sit still. Mrs. Green ended up making me sit at the long table in the front corner of the room where she could keep a closer eye on my wigglings.

That's one of her forms of punishment. You have to sit there where everybody stares and whispers about you.

But I was so excited that I didn't even care. Let them smirk at me. Horse-owners don't care about little things like that.

I practically pushed the bus all the way home, and I was standing by the front window the last three blocks. It was already three-thirty. What if the horse man came early? Or what if he came late? That would be worse. Or what if he didn't come at all?

I checked in with Mrs. Birdsall, then ran over to Kimberley's to get the sheet-ribbon and the tag. Then Kimberley and I sat on my front steps for several years till it was four o'clock.

Only an hour till Mom got home. What if the horse guy was late? What if . . .

A truck turned into the Perfect Paradise road and started coming slowly toward us. Kimberley and I ran out and waved, and the truck stopped right by our driveway.

"Zelda Hammersmith?" the man asked. It sounded like the same voice I'd talked to on the phone. I was jumping up and down so hard that I could barely answer him.

Slowly he climbed out and said, "That'll be seventeen dollars."

I handed him my quarter bank. "I

couldn't get it open," I told him. "Just take the whole bank."

He stared at me, muttered something I couldn't understand, and tossed the bank into the truck.

Then he walked around to the back and let down the tailgate. "One horse, coming up," he said cheerfully.

Out of the blackness came our horse.

He was huge and dirty, a sort of faded-cream color, with feet that were splayed out and breaking off around the edges. His mane stuck up in wisps, and there were deep hollows above his eyes.

He ambled down the ramp, leaned his chin on my shoulder, and sighed as the truck drove away.

℮

Kimberley stood back from Biscuit and stared at him. "He's so dirty,' she said. Count on Kimberley to notice that.

"He's got green stains on his knees," she went on. "And what are those brown, yukky-looking spots?"

"You don't want to know," I muttered. Biscuit wasn't the cleanest horse I'd ever seen. Well, yes, he was—because he was the only horse I'd ever seen in person, except for the ponies at Holiday Park.

I tried to stand back from him to get a better look, but he kept leaning on my shoulder. I did notice that his back sank way down in the middle, like a very fat person had sat on him and squashed him down. And I could see that he had lots of white hairs all around his nose and eyes, and that his eyes had a kind of milky glaze to them.

It occurred to me that Biscuit might be past his prime.

Oh, well, he was a horse, and time was passing. I tied his rope to the porch railing, and Kimberley and I got busy with the sheet-ribbon. We wound it around his neck and tied a big bow up behind his ears. Then, since there was plenty of sheet left, we tied another big bow around his sagging stomach, and a smaller one around his tail. I pinned the H. B. M. card on the biggest part of the stomach bow and stood back to admire the sight.

He was a very . . . well . . . he was a most . . . well . . . he was the most decorated horse I'd ever seen.

Almost five o'clock. Mom would be home any minute now.

Suddenly Kimberley said, "Hey, look at him."

I looked.

Oh, no.

The horse was sagging to his knees, rolling slowly over onto his side. He sighed a very long, deep sigh.

"Don't roll on the bow," I yelled.

I ran to him and grabbed his rope and tried to pull him up. He was deadweight at the end of the rope.

Mrs. Birdsall came out of her trailer and peered down at Biscuit.

"What are you doing with a horse in your yard, child?"

"Trying to wake him up," I snapped. "What does it look like I'm doing?" I knew that was smarty-talk and not to be tolerated, but I was too worked up to care.

Other people started walking toward us—Mr. Jacobmeyer and Kimberley's mother and half a dozen others. This would be perfect for yelling "Happy Birthday!" when Mom drove up . . . if only the horse would quit lying there like he was . . .

Oh, no.

OH, NO!

"Your Biscuit isn't rising," Kimberley said. She would make a joke at a funeral. Which, come to think of it, she just had.

I took one more look at Biscuit, hoping I was wrong, but I wasn't.

He was on his way to horse heaven.

This was the worst mess I had ever

been in. I sat down on Biscuit's side and put my determined chin in my hands.

Then, to make the worst even worse, Mom drove up. She jumped out of the car and stared down at Biscuit and me like she couldn't believe her eyes. She probably couldn't.

I looked up and pasted on my best fake smile.

"Happy Birthday, Mom."

ℭ

One thing I've learned in life: When things can't possibly get any worse, they always do.

I tried to explain Biscuit to Mom and ended up crying against her stomach. Before she could get me simmered down, the Perfect Paradise manager got there and started dancing around, yelling about how no pets, especially no dead horses, were allowed in Perfect Paradise.

Then from out of nowhere a City

Health Department car drove up, and
the officer said there'd been a report of
a dead horse. Was it a mistake? No . . .
obviously Biscuit was very real.

There were city health codes and
regulations about dead horses on lawns
in residential areas, he told us. Mom
explained things over my bawling head,
and somehow the whole mess got sorted
out. The health man called a dead-stock
removal truck, and Biscuit left us,
trailing ribbons of glory and a bed-sheet
behind him.

At the last minute, Mom darted out
and pulled off the H. B. M. card to keep
as a memento.

Gradually everyone went home,
talking about that crazy Zelda Hammersmith, and Mom and I went inside.
She kicked off her shoes and got us
each a Mountain Dew. Then we sat on
the sofa and stared at each other.

"Well," she said finally, "this was,
without a doubt, the most exciting and
memorable birthday I have ever had."

I started bawling again. "I wanted to give you such a great present. I wanted to make your childhood dream come true."

She grinned and pulled me into a big hug. "Well, hon, you did all that. You gave me a horse, though I will never know how you managed to buy one for seventeen dollars."

I decided not to tell her that part.

"I didn't exactly get a lot of use out of him," she went on carefully, "but at least I did own a horse for a while there."

"A dead horse," I bellowed.

She handed me the Kleenex box.

"Yes, but you didn't buy me a dead horse. You have to remember that. You bought me an elderly horse who just happened to be so near the pearly gates that the truck ride over here was too much for him, and he went to his great reward at an unfortunate moment."

I nodded. It didn't sound quite so bad that way.

She went on. "The main thing to remember here is that you spent a lot of time and effort, and every penny you had, to try to give me something I wanted very much. And what you gave me was even better than a dead horse."

I looked up hopefully.

"You gave me proof that I have raised a thoughtful and loving human being."

"I also gave you a cleaned-out shed," I added.

"That's true. You did. So all in all, it's been a wonderful birthday, and I thank you for your efforts."

That night while we washed the supper dishes, I said, "Mom, it's only six more shopping weeks till Christmas. Do you have any ideas what you might like?"

"Nothing alive," she yelled. "Nothing that used to be alive! Nothing that ever might be alive!"

I haven't decided yet what her Christmas surprise is going to be, but it will be something really great.

5. Zelda, the Private Ear

There was trouble in Paradise. I don't mean the real paradise where you go after you die. I mean Perfect Paradise Trailer Park.

The trouble was Beth Ann Smith.

Before Beth Ann moved in, Kimberley and I were the only fourth-graders who lived there, so we were best friends. I didn't have to do anything to keep Kimberley as my best friend. It was automatic.

But all of a sudden, Beth Ann moved in. She and Kimberley took one look at each other, and that was that. They were instantly better friends than Kimberley and I were. And it was easy to see why.

Beth Ann took dance lessons. Tap and ballet, just like Kimberley. It was sickening to watch them standing by Kimberley's porch railing, one arm curled over their heads, one leg stuck out in toe-pointy position, trying to impress each other.

And although Beth Ann wasn't as neat as Kimberley (nobody is as neat as Kimberley), she did have something going for her. She had a color scheme.

Pink.

Everything she wore was pink. She even had pink jeans, and if that doesn't make you sick, she also had pink frames on her glasses. She said she was going to get pink braces on her teeth next year, but I didn't believe that one. Still, it goes to show you how pink a person she was, and there has to be something wrong with someone like that. Right?

At first, when the two of them started doing everything together, I felt a little bit left out. Then I felt more left out. Then I started getting really worried. If Kimberley had Beth Ann, then all I'd have was Derek, and he was awful. He was too little to do anything, and he always had to go home just when the fun was starting. Besides, he hadn't learned to blow his nose yet. Nobody wants to hang around with a face that looks like that.

Things might not have been so bad if it hadn't been summer. You have to have a best friend to do stuff with in summer, or you might as well not bother to get up in the morning. And now, my formerly dependable—boring but dependable—best friend suddenly wasn't, anymore. Now she was Beth Ann's best friend, and it looked like they were going to spend three months with their right hands on a porch rail and their left toes pointed.

It all came to a boil on Friday when

I showed up at Kimberley's after lunch. I was all cleaned up and ready to go to the mall. We always went to the big shopping mall in the city on Friday afternoons with Kimberley's mother. It was the best part of the week. Her mother would turn us loose to get rid of us. Then we'd meet her by the fountain at four. If she was in a good mood, she'd give us money for caramel corn.

I always had to lick my hand after caramel corn and then wipe it on my leg. If I didn't, it would be so sticky that I'd collect little bits of fuzz and paper scraps everywhere I went.

Kimberley could eat an entire bag of caramel corn without any of it touching her skin. Isn't that amazing?

But the point isn't caramel corn. The point is this: Going to the mall with Kimberley and her mother on Friday afternoons was my right as a human being. Especially if the mall was having something like a petting zoo or a display of camping trailers.

So I was not expecting to be stabbed in the back and speared in the heart. But that's what happened. I got to Kimberley's at the regular time on Friday, and her older brother said they'd already gone.

To the mall.

Kimberley and her mother.

And Beth Ann.

I yelled at him that they were supposed to take *me,* and he yelled back that Beth Ann told Kimberley that Zelda didn't want to go this time. Then he yelled that I should quit yelling at him, because it wasn't his fault.

No. It wasn't his fault. It was a snake in the grass. A lying, pink snake in the grass of Perfect Paradise, and I was going to have to step on her. Somehow.

I decided not to talk it over with Mom that night. I figured she'd give me some good advice like "Be patient," and I didn't want good advice.

I wanted revenge.

As I lay in bed with the dark all around me, I could hear voices from the trailer next to ours. Mrs. Birdsall was having company, and I could hear every word they said. Of course any friend of Mrs. Birdsall's would be boring, so their talk wasn't worth listening to. But it did give me an idea.

What if I were a detective, I thought, starting to get excited. I could listen outside Beth Ann's trailer and try to find out something bad about her, so Kimberley would drop her. I could be like a private eye on television, only I'd be listening instead of peeking through keyholes.

Zelda, the private ear.

I fell asleep smiling.

℮

The next night was perfect for spying, because it was Saturday night, and Mom always watches "The Saturday Night Movie" at eight o'clock. That meant she wouldn't notice that I was still outside after dark.

Kimberley and her whole family were gone. On Saturday nights they always have supper with her grandma, so that was perfect, too. Beth Ann was home, and so were her parents. All I had to do was wait till Derek's mother called him in at eight, and after that I had the place to myself.

The sun was setting when I started my approach. And no one could see me anyway because I was wearing my detective outfit: dark jeans, my fastest tennis shoes, a dark long-sleeved sweater, and my mom's best black silk scarf to cover my hair. Luckily Mom had been on the phone when I sneaked out, or she would have caught me. I probably looked like a refugee from a war-torn country, but at least my light skin and hair were covered up so I could go spying in the dark.

I circled around the target, the

Smiths' trailer, and tiptoed close to it from behind their tool shed. I flattened down and crawled between the back of the trailer and a row of low bushes just a foot or so from the metal trailer skirting. It was perfect.

Beth Ann and her parents were in the living room watching television. I peeked in, saw where everyone was, and then dropped down to a listening position.

All I heard was television music. I could have stayed home and heard that. I began to have the sinking feeling this wasn't going to work. Beth Ann probably had no dark, horrible secrets. *She'd be just the type,* I grumbled to myself. You can't depend on anyone these days.

Finally the program was over, and someone turned off the television. In the stillness I heard something odd—a soft, high, crying sound, like a far-off baby.

Mrs. Smith said, "Beth Ann, good night now."

And like the perfect, pink daughter she was, Beth Ann got up and kissed them both good night—I could hear the smacks—and went to her room.

I tried to turn around to crawl toward her bedroom, but did you ever try to turn around on your hands and knees in a foot-wide space without making any noise?

I scrambled and bumped.

Suddenly something grabbed me from behind.

I started to yell, but I caught myself in time. I croaked instead. The thing that had me by the hair wasn't a hand; it was just a branch of bush. But it had my mom's best black silk scarf, and it wasn't going to let go.

Above my head, the window opened wider, and Mr. Smith said, "I thought I heard something out there."

He was right over me! I pressed against the trailer and hid my pale hands so I'd be completely dark and invisible in the bushes.

"Probably just a dog," Mrs. Smith said from farther back in the room.

Just then, from down the row of trailers, I heard Mom's voice. "Zelda, come on in now."

I was in trouble.

Mr. Smith backed away from the window, and I started trying to unsnag the scarf without tearing it. While I worked, I heard Mrs. Smith.

"Oh, James, I meant to tell you. I've got a buyer for the black-marked baby. A nice couple from Independence. They're coming tomorrow night at eight to see him."

Black-marked baby? What was that? I wondered. If they had a baby, it would explain that funny little crying sound. But how could they sell a baby, and what were the black marks?

Odder and odder.

I finally got the scarf loose and crawled to the corner and bolted for home. I stuck the scarf under my sweater in hopes of getting past Mom.

I wasn't sure the night's detecting had gotten me anything useful, but I was sure going to look into this baby-selling business.

ে

I got up early the next morning and decided to surprise Mom with breakfast in bed. She worked hard all week at the sausage factory, and it would be nice to give her a treat. And I could ask her about black-marked babies while she ate. It would be better if I didn't tell her about the spying. I'd been in enough trouble with her lately.

I decided on pancakes. They were her favorite Sunday breakfast. How hard could it be to make pancakes when the recipe was right there on the box?

The directions said to put in eggs. If they meant eggs without shells, they should have said so. All they said was put in two eggs, and I did. I mashed them up so they wouldn't be lumpy, but I didn't remember Mom's pancakes having all those shell hunks sticking up.

And the directions on the box didn't say how to tell when the bottoms of the pancakes were done. Smoke started coming from around the edges, so I turned them over. They were a little blacker than Mom's pancakes.

I didn't know how to work the Mr. Coffee machine, so I made hot chocolate. It was more or less the right color, but crumbs of chocolate powder kept popping up on top. I got so mad at those crumbs that I whammed them with the spoon, and the cup broke.

But after a while I had a nice breakfast on a tray, with a bouquet of dandelions in a Bugs Bunny glass. I kicked open Mom's bedroom door and said, "Surprise!"

She was surprised.

But she wasn't very hungry.

I sat on the bed trying not to bounce while she poked at her pancakes and sipped carefully at the hot chocolate, getting chocolate powder on her lip.

"Mom," I said finally, "can a baby have black marks on it?"

"What?"

It takes her a while to get alert in the morning. I repeated the question.

She shook her head. "Where did you get that?"

I shrugged. "I just heard it, on television, I guess. Somebody said he was going to sell a black-marked baby. I wondered if you could sell your baby if there was something wrong with it, like black marks."

Then she laughed. "Oh, you mean the black *market*. Sometimes criminals steal babies from people and sell them illegally, and that's called the black market. Because it's illegal, see?"

Criminals? I perked up. "How would they do it?"

Mom looked at me suspiciously, but went on. "Oh, I suppose it's usually a

ring of crooks. They might steal somebody's baby and then pretend it belonged to a relative who couldn't keep
it. They'd say they were offering it for
adoption, but really they were selling it.

"Then a couple who wants children
adopts the baby, or something like that.
I don't know. Why are you so interested, Zelda?"

I thought it was terrible that anyone would steal babies, but I had to play
it cool, like a real detective. Mom can
very often look right into my head and
see what's going on in there. I got up
and took her tray.

"I was just curious. I'll wash the
breakfast dishes now," I said. I got out
of there hoping she'd go back to sleep,
and she did.

I made myself some toast and then
tried to wash the burned-up pancake
pan. The black stuff was on there like
cement. Finally I buried the whole thing
at the bottom of the garbage bag and
went outside.

The more I thought about the Smith business, the more sure I was that Mom was right. They were a black-market baby-selling ring. I should have known when I heard a fake-sounding name like Smith. And once Kimberley found out . . . hooray!

But first things first. Zelda Hammersmith, Private Ear, would have to bust the crime ring.

I'd never been in a police station before. I was hoping for jail cells and prisoners acting like caged tigers, but there was only a high counter with a policewoman behind it.

She wore a tight blue jacket with important-looking gold decorations, and she had a steely look in her eye. I was satisfied with her.

"What's your problem? Lose your bike?" she asked.

I stood up as tall as I could. She obviously didn't know with whom she was dealing.

"I am Zelda Hammersmith, and I want to report a ring of crooks selling black-market babies at the Perfect Paradise Trailer Park."

She stared at me for a minute, and then she threw back her head and roared with laughter. I got mad. "I'm not kidding you," I yelled. Two policemen in a back room looked out.

The woman straightened her face as if she'd just remembered policewomen aren't supposed to laugh. "All right, I'll go along with you," she said. "Give me your evidence."

"Aren't you going to ask me to come into your office?" I demanded.

She ushered me into the back office like she was taking me seriously, but I caught her winking at the men.

With great dignity I said, "Mr. and Mrs. James Smith, at Lot 44, Perfect Paradise Trailer Park, are selling black-market babies. I'm not sure if they're the ones who do the stealing. You'll have to find that out yourself. They have a daughter named Beth Ann, but she's probably a fake. She's the pink one.

"Last night I heard Mrs. Smith, or whatever her real name is, telling Mr. Smith, or whatever his real name is, that she had a buyer for the black-market baby—a nice family from Independence. She said the buyers were coming tonight at eight o'clock to look at the baby. So all you have to do is go there, and you can catch them. Is there any reward?" That last idea had just occurred to me.

The policewoman made some scribbles on a note pad. Then she swept me toward the door with her hand. "I don't know, Miss Hammersmith," she said. "But we do thank you for your information, and we'll be in touch if we need you again."

I looked at her out of the corner of my eye to see if she was winking at the men again, but I couldn't be sure.

All the way home, I had the depressing feeling that she'd been kidding me along. She probably didn't even write down what I told her. I could hardly wait to get older so people would start taking me seriously.

One thing was clear. If the crooks were going to get caught in the act of selling that baby tonight, it was going to be up to me to catch them.

$\mathcal{C}$

My plan was simple. All the great plans of history have been simple. That's part of their beauty. I knew I was going to need help to capture the Smiths, and I decided to get it in the most simple and direct way I knew.

I sat on my front steps from seven o'clock on, watching and waiting and planning. Things looked good. Two trailers down, Mr. Jacobmeyer was washing his car. Someone else was mowing the lawn, and at the far end of the street two older boys had their heads under the hood of a car.

But as eight o'clock got closer, the

lawn-mowing person went inside, and the two boys slammed the car hood down and disappeared. Even Mr. Jacobmeyer was at the polishing stage of washing his car, so he wouldn't be around much longer.

By seven minutes after eight, I was getting worried. What if the baby-buyers didn't show up? What if they'd gotten wind of the crime ring and chickened out? What if . . .

Then they drove in. I could tell they were the buyers because the lady was carrying a cardboard box with a blue blanket folded in it. Probably to carry the baby in. My heart started racing, just like in books when the heroine is in danger.

I waited till they'd gone inside the Smiths' trailer. Then I sneaked up beside the screen door and listened. I didn't dare look, or they'd have seen me. But I heard plenty.

I heard the baby crying its tiny newborn-baby cry, and the woman from

Independence was saying, "Oh, isn't he precious? Harold, I want him. Let's buy him. Please, honey. He's just so precious I could die."

Well, anybody silly enough to buy a black-market baby would talk that way, I supposed.

And Mrs. Smith was just as bad. "Oh, he's my precious little baby," she cooed. Sickening.

It was time. Now!

I turned and ran down the middle of the street yelling, "Help, fire! Help, police! Help! Murderers!"

I liked that last one the best, so I yelled louder.

"Help! Murderers!" I shrieked.

Mr. Jacobmeyer's polishing rag flew into the air.

Doors slammed. People came running out of every trailer. Mom and Mrs. Birdsall and Kimberley's family. Everyone. It was great.

I ran back up the street toward the Smiths' with the whole train of them following me. Suddenly there was music to my ears . . . a police siren?

The policewoman had taken me seriously after all! This was my finest hour.

With two blue uniforms close behind me, I jerked open the Smiths' screen door and yelled, "Stop! You're under arrest!"

Did you ever play a game called "statues," where somebody swings you around by the arm and yells, "Freeze," and you have to freeze in exactly that position? That's what the five people in the Smiths' living room looked like.

The buyer couple stood next to Mr. and Mrs. Smith, and Beth Ann stood pinkly behind them.

And in the cardboard box, nestled in the blue blanket, was . . . a kitten.

A *kitten.*

With black marks on its face and paws.

That's when I knew I was in the worst trouble of my whole life.

I tried to shrink down and slip away behind the bushes, but a hand caught me. This time it was a real hand, not a bush. It was Mom's hand, and she had me by the scruff of my neck just like a mother cat . . . but I didn't want to think about kittens just then. "All right, Zelda Marie," she boomed, "what is this all about?"

I was trying to explain when one of the policemen bent down to get a closer look at my face. "Hey," he said to his partner. "Isn't that the squirrelly kid who pretended she was run over by a car one time?"

I pulled my head down in my collar like a turtle and tried to smile.

"Just a little joke, folks. Sorry."

Mr. Jacobmeyer stomped away grumbling. A few of the others said things about undisciplined children who shouldn't be allowed to run loose. The policeman gave me a talking-to about filing false police reports and getting a juvenile record.

Mom just marched me home. But after she got over being mad about my disturbing the peace and almost getting innocent people arrested, she did give me a chance to explain.

"Next time," she said, "get your facts straight before you go jumping into things. And next time, don't go listening outside people's windows. And next time, *there will not be a next time, Zelda Marie.*"

Actually there was no need for a next time. Beth Ann told Kimberley I was the weirdest person she'd ever met, and she never wanted to have anything to do with me, ever again.

Kimberley told her that I wasn't all that bad, and that I was really an interesting person to have as a best friend, because at least I wasn't boring.

Beth Ann said, well, if that's the kind of person you want for a friend, you don't want *me,* and Kimberley said that's okay with me, Beth Ann, I was getting tired of looking at pink all the time anyway.

So Kimberley and I are best friends again.

And the Smiths are moving to a quieter trailer park.

෴

And I'm never going to get in trouble again!